AN AETHERIAL WAR SHORT STORY COLLECTION

An Aetherial War Short Story Collection

Volume 1

NATHAN EARL DOVERSPIKE

Nathan Earl Doverspike

This wouldn't be possible without the encouragement and support from my parents, loving wife, and amazing friends. To Jaina, never stop believing in yourself and striving to be great. Your dreams are never too far out of reach.

Never forget: we do what we must.
Because we must.

May the Aether guide your way, Wanderer.

CONTENTS

| 1 |

The First Domino Falls

Approximately Ten Years Before the Events of Book 1: Chaos and Consequences

"Woah, slow down. Tell me again, what happened?" crackled the young male voice over the secure communication through Joren Steel's *tac-com*. The man, a person whom Joren considered the only being remotely resembling a friend at the precinct at which he worked, was Anders Fluery, though he preferred the nickname 'Snowman' was projected above the minute device strapped to his left wrist. His short black hair and fatty face made him look even older than the twenty-five years he had been alive. Joren was almost old enough now to be his father, but that didn't stop him from treating him more akin to a friend. Snowman was proficient in telemetry, using the Grid to extrapolate their exact address and was often pulled into Joren's cases to assist in identifying where their targets were hiding. Joren didn't know how telemetry worked, nor did he care.

All Joren knew at this moment, was his world had been shattered into a million pieces.

Joren fought against the urge to scream *NO!* He attempted to control his breathing and center his chaotic mind. Nothing was going to bring her back, and nothing was going to heal that gaping wound.

Focus. If there is any way Snowman could use his fancy computer skills to help, he needs to know what happened, even if I can't stand to provide specific details.

"They did it. They said that there would be consequences if I didn't stop, and I stopped. I wasn't providing any assistance to Aetherials or their supporters. I saw it on the surveillance cameras I installed just in case they decided to drop by. Some G.I. elite soldiers came here while I was at the office, and they..." He choked down his words, unable to finish the sentence. There was a long pause in the conversation. Neither said anything and besides the whizzing of traffic outside his apartment, the only other noise was soft clicking as Snowman furiously typed away.

Finally, after what seemed like an eternity, Snowman interrupted the solemn silence. "Do you have any recordings of her? Anything with her likeness and voice?"

He looked at the small curved *tac-com* across his wrist. He had a few recordings of her, but nothing too extensive. Never in a million years could he have imagined this day would pass. The handful he had would have to do, though. "Yeah, a couple. Why?"

"Good. I'm sending you an address. This is all off the record so tell anyone, and I'll deny we ever spoke about this. I'll tell them you've gone AWOL and you'll never see me again. I'm scrubbing this call from the G.I. database as soon as we hang up. Meet me at this address tonight. Bring every electronic trace you have of her. Except her, of course. That would be weird, and I'm into some weird stuff, but not that. Anyway, I have a program I've been working on for years, and it's time I tested it out for real. This is the perfect chance to see if it works as I designed it. Plus, if it does, it should somewhat help with your situation." An indicator that looked like a rectangular page with two straight lines portraying text on the bottom of his *tac-com* lit up blue from the incoming message notification. Joren touched a shaking finger against the icon and read it to himself.

Rock Bottom, Lower Levels, D39 @ 22:00 standard time

He knew the place. Some seedy bar that was fixed up decades ago by a synth with good intentions but not a lot of money. "Yeah, sure. I'll bring what I have and meet you there."

"Copy that. And Joren, for whatever it's worth, I agree with what you've been doing. You didn't deserve what happened to you."

He hated that phrase 'didn't deserve what happened'. It meant nothing. They were nothing more than empty words. Nothing would make it right. Nothing would bring back his little princess. He didn't respond verbally; instead giving Snowman a nod and ended the call with a deliberate press of a button on the device.

The middle-aged broken man sat back in his chair in darkness and silence. Normally, the silence would be a welcome reprieve from the constant commotion in the local office where he was a detective for the Galactic Imperium. At night, he would have enjoyed putting his daughter to sleep after enjoying dinner and shows on their Holovid together.

Now, the silence was deafening, maddening even, and nothing would make it disappear. His knuckles cracked and turned white as he clenched them in indescribable rage. Even the occasional hum and lights illuminating the dark room from vehicles shooting by his skyrise apartment on Coropolis did little to take his mind away from the pain. He brought up the recordings option on his *tac-com* menu floating in front of him, and clicked the one titled "tenth birthday".

Her image appeared instantly in front of him, as innocent and lively as the day the moment was captured. Her smile was infectious as she twirled around in her new dress. Its white color with gold roses woven into it made a golden ring as she threw her arms out and spun in clumsy circles. A beautiful laugh, just slightly louder than a giggle, reverberated in the near-empty room from the projection. He would have wept if it weren't for his eyes running out of tears to shed earlier in the night. Instead, the abyss in his stomach sunk deeper and his heart froze over.

Joren took a lengthy swig from the cylindrical glass bottle that he had retrieved from his pantry not long before he called Snowman. The brown fluid within the Leviathan branded bottle was familiar with its strong scent and taste. It didn't eliminate the pain, but he hoped it would numb it, even for a moment or two. It burned on the way down, but the spiced rum also had a smoothness to it that spoke to its quality and lofty price tag.

'For when life tries to swallow you whole' was printed under the Leviathan brand. It was a catchy slogan, and he almost laughed at the accuracy. Almost. His mind only drifted so far from reality.

They stole EVERYTHING from me. She was the only person left I cared about in this dumpster fire of a galaxy. If they think this is going to be the end of me, they will be sorely disappointed. This is only the beginning. If no one else stands up, I'll be that person.

I'll burn them down from the inside. I'll be the first domino to fall that brings down the Galactic Imperium's reign. If it's the last thing I do, I'll still be the one to put the plan in motion. This crime will not go unpunished.

My sweet princess, I will avenge you.

Joren's head spun as he took another swig of the savory spiced rum and began playing another of the few recordings he had left of his little Ava. It was going to be the longest night of his life, and he needed some liquid comfort to make it through. Tear d slid quickly down his ghostly expression, eager to reach safety from the rage building inside the widowed father.

They. Will. Pay. He promised solemnly in the unusually quiet night on Coropolis.

| 2 |

Of Magic and Man

Ten years before the events of Chaos and Consequences

Just a little bit more. No, that's too far. Crank it back half a turn counter-clockwise. Slowly, slowly. Almost there. Ah-ha! Got it!

"Are you sure this – device – or whatever the hell it is, will work? I mean, the man's basically dead. Wouldn't we be better off dumping him behind the building and moving on?" The Galactic Imperium soldier remarked sarcastically behind Tu'Mar. His uniform was the standard military-issued white outfit with gold trim on the top of the matching white boots, pant pockets, breastplate, and around the crease on his shoulder. His short blonde hair was as slick as his tongue, which he used too often. The single star under the Galactic Imperium emblem would normally lead one to believe he was a lower rank soldier, but the disgusting arrogance that coated every word indicated otherwise.

Tu'Mar suppressed her rising annoyance with this simple-minded fool. "I was instructed by your superior to follow through with the creation of this highly sophisticated Aetherial core. Your simple human mind cannot begin to comprehend the scope of complexity required to make this scientific breakthrough, let alone make it work properly. Human minds are much too, what's the word, *barbaric* for this level of expertise." She remarked as she continued working tirelessly.

Her insult must have touched a nerve, and the cold steel of his rifle's barrel pressed firmly against her large Praugian head. Her first instinct was to jump out of the way, but she knew any sign of weakness would only push her luck. The Praug didn't typically believe in luck, but if there was such a thing, she had very little left to spare.

"I won't dance around the reality of our situation with fancy words, alien. You fuck this up and you'll be six feet under faster that that poor bastard on the table. Hell, judging by the lack of color in your weird face he's feeling better than you are." The barrel of the rifle pushed hard against her head before the cold metal retreated to the soldier's side.

I beg to differ about who the real aliens are in this galaxy, invader. We were here for tens of thousands of years before your belligerent, war-loving breed appeared. I'd say go back to where you came from, but even if you hadn't forgotten where that was, you couldn't go back if you wanted to.

Focus Tu'Mar. This needs to be right or it'll be my time to sit at the table with the old gods. You were sent here for a reason, and this is it. Bring to life that which has no meaning or purpose. Give this man a meaning. Give him a purpose. Just as Joren Steel gave you when you needed one.

The Praug wiped her orange four-fingered hands on her blue science coat. The webbing between her fingers made swimming a breeze, however , as they secreted water whenever she was under duress, they often interfered with her projects She blinked her large eyes as she calmed her nerves and the gills on her neck, along with her slanted nostrils flared.

"You aliens are downright disgusting. I'm sure you've heard that many times, but figured you could hear it one more time before you're dead." His hand slapped against his peers in a motion the humans called a 'high five'. It made a horrible clapping noise that made all the Praug in the room shudder slightly. Despite the bad reputation that Rhonar often got, and sometimes deservingly so, Humans were the true epitome of brutes. Only one human had ever treated her with a molecule of decency, and he was long gone. She wished she would see him again one day, but that day would likely never come.

Refocus. You're so close to completing it. Just another minor adjustment here, and another one there. By the will of the gods, I hope this works.

Tu'Mar slightly straightened one of the myriads of small Duratanium metal bars woven together in a hexagonal shape with an emerald green crystal set in the middle. Although how it worked remained a mystery, Duratanium, a cobalt tinted metal, had unique properties that gave it the ability to conduct Aether at an atomic level. Aetherials once coveted the precious metal before their kind was all but eliminated. Now that they were no longer around to hoard it, the Praug were happy to take it off their hands. So were the Galactic Imperium, who were adamant on figuring out its secrets in the secluded research facility they were currently in. Unfortunately for the Praug, the military prowess of the Galactic Imperium gave them little choice but to cooperate.

Still, it was better than the alternative.

"There! My calibrations are complete and it is done." Tu'Mar took a step back, a wide smile spread across her face as she gave herself a front-row seat to admire her work. Amidst dozens of small steel tools, wires, and bits of crystal, sat the first of its kind and previously believed to be more impossible to create in practice than in theory: an artificial Aetherial Core.

"About damn time. Put it in the half-dead man and see if it actually works. Then, we can talk about your payment. *If* it actually works." He said with a scoff and a sarcastic chuckle.

Her smile faded as quickly as it came with the sudden realization that she wasn't sure it would work the way she intended. It could bring the man back to life for seconds, and instantly fail. It could simply not work at all. Science was a form of art to the Praug and their self-worth often rested on their scientific abilities. Some excelled in discovering cures to diseases, others were great at inventing improvements for agriculture and mining. In her not-so-humble opinion, Tu'Mar considered herself an Aetherial prodigy.

Webbed hands trembling, she lifted the core from the table, and walked it over to the prom man on the cold, metal operating table. The dark-skinned man had a gaping hole in his chest where once his heart beat, now a the glowing emerald core and cobalt-blue rings rotated around rhythmically. His black hair was pulled back in neat dreadlocks; his creased brows and slight wrinkles by his eyes aged him at roughly forty or so years old, though his impeccable muscle tone and physique implied otherwise. He was alive, though barely. The machinery kept him in a catatonic state as Tu'Mar worked tirelessly for the last eight standard days, taking breaks to quickly devour her meals and then promptly returning to work. Holovids beside the bed projected his various vitals to ensure he was still among the living while she worked.

This man was the cause of her sleep deprivation, building anxiety, and a number of other maladies. And yet, he was about to be her ticket to freedom. And immortal glory.

She gently placed the core within his chest as her hands began to sweat again. Praug were naturally resistant to bacterial residue, so she didn't bother wearing gloves while working on live specimen. One tiny plug after another, she disconnected it from the machine and prayed it would work. With the final plug removed, she stepped back, waiting for it to spark to life.

It didn't.

"Well, looks like your freak experiment failed. Time to go out back."

Tu'Mar shook her head in disbelief. *It didn't work? How didn't it work? I calibrated everything to match the Aetherial wavelengths he was outputting. It's scientifically impossible for this core to not work.*

A firm hand grabbed her arm above the shoulder and yanked, hard. She fell backward, arms flinging in front of her as she crashed to the floor. She struggled as a second hand grabbed her other arm and she was dragged across the smooth floor. Arms waving, legs kicking, she fought with all the strength her slim figure could muster. Praug weren't known for their physical prowess, and she was on the lighter side of her species.

"Let me go! I'm sure it's just a simple adjustment and I'll have it working. I give you my word it'll work this time."

"You gave your word already, and in exchange, we spared your life. We aren't in the business of handing out free donations. Your time is up, science freak." The automatic door sensors, detecting the Galactic Imperium soldiers dragging her out.

Vroom. Before they could leave, a sound that could only be compared to an engine bursting through a planet's atmosphere deafened everyone in the room. The scientists and soldiers alike struggled to gather their senses. The man, once a lifeless science experiment, slowly sat up on the table. His movement appeared almost robotic, with a twinge of hesitation as he blinked, taking in his chaotic surroundings.

The man cautiously glanced down at his chest for an extended moment. He stared into the core as it hummed with power. Aetherial energy danced around and seemed to radiate from that emerald crystal within; the Duratanium rings rotated around it in an indistinguishable rhythmic pattern like a planet rapidly revolving around a sun without an end in sight.

"Who am I? What am I?" His deep voice asked. His eyes jumped between everyone in the room before they fixed on Tu'Mar. He blinked twice and tilted his head slightly in confusion.

Shaking with excitement, Tu'Mar scrambled to her feet as the guard dropped his gun and jaw simultaneously. His counterpart swore aloud in awe at the successful merging of magic and man before them.

I did it! I knew I could do it all along. You may have doubted my genius, mother, but I never lost faith.

I told you it was possible.

She replied excitedly, "Your name is Malik Maholmes, and you are the first of your kind. We have a lot to talk about."

| 3 |

Operation Codename: Stormbringer

Minutes before Operation Codename: Stormbringer begins

Few things thrilled him more than the hunt. The hunt to bring down criminals posing a threat to the Galactic Imperium, and those within its protection. The hunt of those running from the grasp of justice, running from their inevitable fate. Running, from him.

Resting amid the myriad of small robotics in his chest that were keeping him alive was a thin blue cable. As he plugged the cable into a matching port on the front of his holovid, a smile crossed his face. Just this month, he had apprehended three more criminals aiding in hiding Aetherials, he even managed to catch and kill one of those bastards. They may be magical, but they certainly weren't omnipotent or immortal. That, he was sure of.

The holovid blinked to life, showing his vital signs as stable. No anomalies remained from the damage his body sustained in his last encounter with an Aetherial a few days prior. The technologically advanced power core that energized the mechanical limbs attached to his body was fully charged. He unplugged it, let the cable retract on its own into its little compartment, and then donned a black shirt that he had hanging in his closet. Never one for fashion, he had a plethora of black shirts in there, as well as his Galactic Imperium armor, modified plasma pistols resting in their leather holsters, and shoes, which he had taken pride in shining the night before. No one except the bio-mechanical doctors who pieced him back together eighteen years ago had ever seen him fully unarmored. He planned to keep it that way.

A soft beep from the device implanted within his left ear alerted him to an incoming communication. He pressed an inconspicuous button below his ear and greeted them. "Captain Demico here. What are the leads today?"

A gentle but firm female voice responded. "Good morning, Captain Demico. I hope this communication doesn't disturb you too early."

Never too early, if it involves-

"We have an Aetherial sighting, Captain. Two soldiers reported they ran into one of them yesterday." She said, without waiting for a response. "Spotted outside a dilapidated bar called...what the hell was its name...oh yeah, *Rock Bottom*. It's down on the ground level of District Thirty-Nine. Facial recognition was only able to pull up a name and where the Grid lists him as residing. According to the records we could pull, his name is supposedly Kai Stormbringer, a middle-aged Human male who we have traced to a large multi-species apartment complex a couple of blocks away from that same bar. We believe he is still at this apartment complex as we speak."

Of course, this Stormbringer would be hiding there! It was so obvious, that it was incredible he hadn't thought to start checking all the local watering holes for wanted traitors to the Galactic Imperium. Their numbers must be so minuscule that they are getting desperate and careless. Then again, if I were wanted by the most impressive military force the galaxy has ever witnessed, I would probably be drinking my life away, too. I wonder if this is the last of the Aetherials. I hope not, because the hunts sure are exciting!

"Thank you, Rodriguez. Ready my squad. E.T.A. is twenty; we will depart for District Thirty-Nine in twenty-five. Mission is Codename: Stormbringer."

"Roger that. E.T.A. is twenty and I will personally make sure they are prepped and ready for Operation Codename: Stormbringer. Rodriguez out." Aetherials could be a tricky foe, should the squad not be completely prepared for all possibilities. Their varying abilities and stages of mastery could make them a Rhonar's plaything, or a deadly combatant.

"Oh, and one more thing Rodriguez."

She paused, a growing hesitation creeping into her voice. "Yes, Captain?"

"Thank you for the good news."

"You're welcome, Captain. See you soon." If he didn't know better, he could have sworn he heard the faintest sight of relief after he graciously showed her gratitude that very few received.

The call disconnected and he was left with only his thoughts as he dazed off for a moment, still staring at his uniform perfectly folded in front of him on a slightly angled display. The black breastplate with gold trim showed signs of wear, but it reminded him of how far he had come since the day everything changed. It had been eighteen years, but not a day went by the fire inside his soul didn't burn to see all Aetherials dead or otherwise disposed of. They were a nuisance, a plague that needed to be eradicated. These vermin needed to be hunted down like the terrifying monsters they were. He didn't just want them dead, he wanted them to suffer like they had made him suffer.

He picked up his reinforced uniform with reconstructed metal hands and pressed it against his chest, making sure to line it up perfectly. What sounded like tiny drills and locks clicking into place could be heard momentarily before he rotated his arms ensuring it was firmly locked in place. Unlike other soldiers, his uniform wasn't just worn, it was part of him, and he was thankful for that. It allowed him to dedicate his life to the one solemn being in this galaxy who gave him a chance to survive and make a difference: The Holy Emperor Tenon.

Next he prepared to put on his similarly colored greaves. He laid them in place and heard the same series of satisfying drills and clicks before he slipped his shined brown boots over them. Unlike other soldiers, he refused to wear protection over his arms, instead electing to intimidate his prey with a clear view of his bulging muscles bearing scars from years of training and hunting. Though they were reconstructed after the attack that nearly took his life all those years ago, they were still the most human part of him, besides his head of course.

The pistol holsters, made of a dark leather, matched his boots and clipped onto each side of his waist. Finally, he retrieved his pistols. Their long barrels and extended plasma magazines allowed him to pour on the firepower while still maximizing the damage of every shot. The fruits of his labor were marked with tallies on the sides of his pistols, and with over twenty tallies between the two golden guns, he was proud of his trophies. Though, as a self-proclaimed hunter, there was never such a thing as too many trophies or a lack of enjoyment in the game.

He was a player in the Aetherial War game, as the common folk called it, and he played to win.

After running his hands through his steel-colored short hair, he deemed himself presentable for the mission ahead. No mirrors would be found in his small apartment, only a bedroom with a closet, a tiny dining area for a single individual, and a toilet with a shower. He didn't need any more reminders of the tragedy so long ago. His hair could be a disheveled mess, and it likely was, but he would never know.

The disfiguration of his face and body still bothered him, but his shiny midnight black helmet helped reestablish his confidence. Though no one dared to utter a word about his appearance to his face, the more people stared the more confident he became that they were terrified of what he hid under his helmet.

He liked it that way.

They knew what he was capable of if they whispered about it in his presence, and it gave him power. He slipped on his helmet, feeling it click into place and suction with an airtight seal. It allowed his damaged eyes to see perfectly through the glowing gold lights that beamed through the midnight black holes. The breathing apparatus assisted his once-punctured lungs to adequately distribute oxygen throughout his bio-mechanical body, even under immense strain. He cracked his knuckles after pulling on his black gloves, the metal fingers letting out a satisfying series of individual *tings* from the motion.

You'd better be ready for the hunt, Stormbringer. Because I am. And I'm coming for you. I hope you put up more of a fight than the last one. They were so disappointing.

He walked out the door, a rare smile on his face under the helmet because today, today was a great day. He had a date with destiny, and its name was Stormbringer.

Let's see how long you last, Stormbringer. Hopefully, you don't disappoint like the last one.

| 4 |

Triple M

Hours after the start of Operation Codename: Stormbringer

DING!

The bell on the coffee brewer loudly alerted Marc that his delectable caffeinated drink was ready to be consumed. It was somewhat of a rarity now; with so many technological advances, hell ships could fly to distant systems hundreds of lightyears away in a matter of weeks through magical wormholes, it was downright a miracle coffee was still around. He figured with all the advancements, there would be mystical pills you consumed to get your coffee fix sated. Well, technically there were, but that wasn't the point. The point was, he was glad there was coffee, and the coffee was ready.

Marc waddled over to the dark brown machine and stubby sausage fingers grabbed the steel cup with steaming black liquid inside. He raised it to his nose, giving it a satisfying and exaggerated snort of aroma before flicking a button to turn off the machine. The red light blinked off, and he smiled while he made his way slowly to his kitchen's cooling unit. It wasn't large, maybe an arm's length wide and a human's torso tall, but it held what he needed. A wave of his flabby hand in front of it made it produce a happy *beep boop* and its front door retracted inside to reveal the chilled contents within. He grabbed the clear glass bottle containing hornless-goat flavored milk, poured an eyeballed tablespoon of it into the steaming beverage, then returned the container to the cabinet. The door shut promptly as he turned to walk away with another satisfying *bleep blop* that sounded like it was saying "thank you" in some coded machine language. Or it was saying "hope you die soon." Either way, he didn't care and kept moving at an overweight snail's pace to his office.

The office was adjacent to the kitchen, which was by design, of course. A converted bedroom, the "office" was a collection of a half dozen holovids mounted to a long wall to his left as he walked in. Instead of clothes where the closet would typically be, he stashed boxes of candy and adrenaline drinks. They were terrible for his health, which he figured already hit rock bottom so it was only uphill from here anyway.

He sat down in the chair facing the holovids, and it groaned from his weight that struggled to stay within the chair without spilling over. The six holovids sprang to life, displaying live feeds from different news channels around the Core. The coffee was still burning hot, but it also helped him focus on any juicy new ongoings. The myriad of beautiful and elegantly dressed news reporters gave their individual takes on the screens before him, which all blended together to Marc. Despite the different stations, they all felt like a singular hive-mind of a channel, trying to inform the uninformed of what they should be aware of, and how they should feel about it.

Unfortunately for the other new sources, that was his job, and he was going to make sure he did it better than any of them. He would also do it in his own unique way.

Marc pressed a couple of buttons on the glowing keyboard in front of him. He read the headlines, pulled up his trusty recording software that featured the most simplistic visual interface imaginable (which was still almost too complicated for his computer-illiterate mind), and made a couple of notes in another program to the right side of the projection.

Aetherials piss off pouty Emperor Tenon
Then destroy a literal underground arena
Before finally escaping with a supposed G. I. defector

Today is going to be a good one, he mused. The man who portrayed a belligerent and often unhinged personality on the Grid glanced at the time on that bottom central holovid, made sure he was comfortable with a few butt wiggles, then pressed a button on his illuminated keyboard resting on the desk in front of him. It was time to go live.

"Welcome to Triple Down with Triple M. If you didn't already realize by now that I'm Triple M, then you should probably go jump off the nearest building, you moron! I've got some real shit to talk to you about today, so if you aren't willing to open your ears and minds, why the hell are you still listening? Go play your virtual games and live your useless life in blissful ignorance."

He coughed a couple of times, swallowing the chunk of phlegm that had dislodged itself and made its way to the top of his throat. The gross pause allowed him to take two more sips of coffee to wash down the mucus before continuing.

"Now, I don't know about you, but whenever I get a chance to piss on the almighty Emperor, I piss as much as possible. From what I'm hearing, it sounds like I'm not the only one. Not one, but TWO Aetherials were spotted on Coropolis yesterday. As if that isn't enough to blow your mind, well get ready for it to completely explode. They got into a tussle with some Captain Douchebag guy, then they *supposedly* killed an innocent civilian in cold blood." He used air quotes for supposedly, though no one could actually see him doing it.

"Okay, well that would usually be enough for me to go on about for a while, but it doesn't stop there folks. They then crashed a local underground, and I mean that in more ways than one, fighting ring and caused some real chaos there. The death toll is still being counted as I speak. Who knows how many bodies they took out in that hell hole?" He had no idea if that was true, but half the "facts" the other reporters were, well reporting, weren't either. It was all a game; he was just another player like everyone else. Another series of coughs occurred followed by more sips of steaming coffee before he continued.

"So that's crazy, right? Two Aetherials in one place, who manage to escape, kill some guy, then trash an underground arena. Well, it doesn't stop there. Turns out, I'm getting reports that they escaped with the help of a defected Galactic Imperium member. That's right, one of the Emperor's own didn't just betray the G.I., but they also took a big smelly dump in their backyard and then rubbed their faces in it! You couldn't write a story this crazy even if you wanted to! I can only imagine the face on big, bad Tenon when he hears about this. I'd bet you ten creds about forty more people are going to be jettisoned into the endless abyss of space after this."

More hacking of phlegm, followed by more sips of his deliciously bitter coffee, before he concluded this section of his show for the morning.

"This has been Mad Marc Maddoc, thanks for listening to Triple Down with Triple M. Maybe you all aren't so bad after all. Or maybe you are a bunch of weird degenerates. Don't know, don't care. Go do something useful now and I'll be back in two standard hours to tell you my opinions on today's happenings and why I'm right."

He pressed a button and stopped the recording, then sat back in his chair, a satisfied smile stretching his flappy cheeks. His coffee was over half empty, and that wasn't going to fly. Triple M needed his piping hot coffee, and the people needed Triple M.

His enlarged body forced a loud creak from the chair as he leaned back and enjoyed his piping hot coffee. *The people need Triple M, and Triple M they will have.*

| 5 |

Choices

Six hours into Operation Codename: Stormbringer

Thump, thump, thump. The Galactic Imperium soldiers boots gently pounded the dusty floor beneath her feet. The shoddy lighting above had allowed her to briefly see a small number of various-sized shadows moving quickly down the tunnel ahead of her. In her excitement at potentially finding the traitors, Cassidy Rodriguez had, as she assumed, nearly trotted quietly enough to catch up to them before they disappeared around another corner of these labyrinthian tunnels without alerting them to her presence. The maze of tunnels beneath Coropolis were a damn headache to navigate, and she couldn't wait until she could breathe some fresh air above ground, even if it was highly sterilized air.

The shadowy figures turned around to face her as she approached, rifle held firmly in her hands but angled as she drew closer.

Damn it, Cas! You really do have lead feet. You were supposed to sneak up on them, not spook them.

Her hands shook fervently as she got a good look at the traitors she was sent to restrain or eliminate, whichever got the job done.

A girl, maybe only a few years younger than herself, met her helmeted gaze with brilliant purple irises. She lacked the horns sprouting from her cranium commonly depicted in the news as well as in games kids would play. Instead, she wore a plain Omnifit shirt with brown sleeves, a lighter blue torso, and a purple "O" on either shoulder. A basic brown belt hugged her waist with two sheaths that held daggers, an odd weapon with such advanced weaponry available. A violet scarf hung around the girl's neck, beautifully matching her eyes. If Cassidy didn't know any better, she would pass by this girl on the streets without a second thought. After all, there were odder things out there than purple irises that sparkled like the stars in the night skies. However, memories surfaced that reminded her of the girl back at the Aetherial man's apartment earlier in the day, and despite that being a complete blur, she realized it was the same girl.

Her eyes darted to the gargantuan beast as it snorted and barred its blocky teeth. This one, she didn't recognize. It wore shiny gold bands around its wrists, tattered pants, toned muscles everywhere she looked, and a Human male breathing shallowly slung over its shoulder. Judging by the soaked shirt and jacket he wore, Cassidy didn't think he had much time left if he didn't receive medical attention soon. He looked like the same guy who blasted a hole in Captain Demico back at the apartment in District 39, but without seeing his face she couldn't be sure. Either way, they were trying to get him help, and she was the only person standing in their way.

Regardless of how hard Cassidy urged her unsteady grip on her gun to settle and at least partially mask the intensity of her nerves, her body had other ideas. Never before had she come face-to-face with such a misfit group of adversaries.

The beast pawed a three-toed scarred hoof at the ground and snorted again, its eyes narrowing on her. She swung her rifle and trained it on the beast, ready to fire if he took even a step forward.

I can't go back empty-handed. No way. Not when I'm this close to getting back to Lieutenant Farseer.

"We were instructed to bring you in, dead or alive. That was an order from Captain Demico. I can't go back empty-handed. You have no idea what he said he would do to us if we didn't find the traitors and bring them into custody."

The girl did her best to persuade Cas as she kept pushing. "I'm sure he was just being dramatic. The G.I. have no reason to send anyone out to the far reaches of the galaxy. I'm sure you know as well as we do, that they are struggling to maintain control of the Core planets as it is. There is no way they would actually carry through with a threat like that. We can forget this ever happened, and go our separate ways. You're providing regular updates on your progress, right? Check-in with them and let them know you haven't found anything."

She was instantly reminded of a moment between herself and Emilee Farseer, or Lieutenant Farseer to most. The beautiful officer had placed a gentle hand on Cas' and looked into her eyes. "Do whatever you need to get back here. Don't you go and get yourself killed down there. Captain Demico is many things, but sane isn't one of them. Whatever you do, make sure you come back in one piece. We will be together once we are honorably discharged."

Her heart ached. She missed Emilee with every fiber of her being. Killing these runaways wasn't going to solve anything. It would just create more paperwork, and paperwork was more time away from her love.

She knew the choice she had to make.

"Fine, you can go. Give me a moment to check in so they don't get suspicious." She pressed a button on the side of her helmet to open a channel with the operator assigned to her team.

A gravelly voice answered loud and clear through her helmet. "Yes, First Class Private Rodriguez. Status?"

Don't sound nervous. Don't sound nervous. Don't sound nervous.

Gathering all her confidence, she said with false conviction, "Northwest tunnels are clear. No sign of the targets."

Mother's blessing, I really hope he buys it.

An audible sigh caught her slightly off guard. She wasn't used to other soldiers showing any emotion, especially not annoyance. Maybe he did buy it?

A moment or two passed, which for Cas felt like an eternity as she reminded herself silently to keep her rifle pointed down so she didn't spook the Rhonar. A crackle came through her helmet and the disgruntled voice responded. "Damnit. Alright, find your way back here. We will regroup and take a different approach. Understood?"

"Roger that. Coming back now to regroup. First Class Private Cassidy Rodriguez out." She stopped holding the button down and slung the rifle back over her shoulder.

"Thank you. You did the right thing."

I didn't do it for you, though. I did it for her. For us. Though I guess I should thank you for not killing me, unlike your friend who looks like karma caught up to him. Funny how the universe works sometimes.

Cassidy Rodriguez nodded. "Thanks for not killing me back at your crazy friend's home. We're even now. I wouldn't come within a lightyear of here from now on. I can't promise my brothers and sisters will be as generous."

Trust me. They won't be.

"Heard you loud and clear. Let's go, Grimhorn. We're almost there."

Without another word, Cassidy turned and marched back towards the Blood Bath Arena, following the navigation displayed inside her helmet with a maze of blue lines and a thicker green line leading the way. As the two groups turned and went their opposite ways, Cas could only think of two things: she hoped she never saw them again and how much she couldn't wait to see Emilee again after this assignment.

I made the choice I had to; I made the only choice that would allow me to survive and see you again. I'm coming, my love. I'll be on my way back in no time.

| 6 |

The Endbringer

Thirty-six hours after the beginning of Operation Codename: Storm-bringer

"I am going to ask you, one…more…time. Where did they go?" The man demanded in a low growl through gritted teeth. He focused his mind on the shirtless man with tattered pants and small circular scars near the veins just above his forearm. A breeze whipped around his dark cape moodily, and the gold trim on it brilliantly reflected the lights high above. He donned a matching midnight black uniform, with the same gold trim on the cuffs and Galactic Imperium insignia stitched on his left breast.

He clenched his fist tighter, his knuckles cracking and the midnight leather glove strained from the pressure. The swirling black Aether tendrils snaking from his fist gripped the man's throat as he clawed at them to no avail. He gasped for air as they increased their stranglehold on his veiny jugular, squeezing what little room was left in it until it closed completely. The man with tattered pants began panicking, throwing his arms out towards his assailant hoping to latch on to his flowing cape, shirt, or anything he could get his hands on to pull himself out of the Aetherial snare.

Above them zoomed ships of all shapes and sizes, transporting beings and cargo from one mundane task or drab location to the next. The neon lights of District 39 flashed advertisements specifically customized to those looking at them with enticing slogans created by creative, and usually morally, bankrupt trillionaires. All that glitz and glamour, and yet this place felt hollow to its core. Beings devoid of meaning, trying desperately to find it in meaningless shows, clubs, bars, drugs, and a number of other less socially acceptable forms of entertainment. If the Endbringer felt anything towards them, it was pity and disgust.

Just as the man choked what would be his last breath, the man in black and gold released the tendrils from his neck. He collapsed into a sobbing fetal position, repeatedly begging for his life to be spared.

"You will tell me what I want to know. And *maybe* I'll let you live," he said once more. His patience was wearing thin, and he knew if he wanted to stay hot on the Aetherial and Demico's trail he had to wrap up this aggressive conversation quickly. The skin and bones beggar must have noticed the quivering lip of annoyance, because he finally gave an answer.

"I don't know. I told you all I know. I swear it on the Holy Mother's Blessing."

"Then we're done here." He raised his hand and spread his fingers; tendrils of pure darkness moved towards the sobbing coward and lifted him into the air with outstretched arms so he could stare into the eyes of the one who would be his final judge. As the prey stared into the dead, black eyes of the Nekrofiend, he flung spittle into the air from more pathetic attempts to save his soul.

"Wait, wait. I remember now! The guy said something about…shit. Four claws? Two claws? No, don't do this. It was Three Claws. Yeah, that's it. They were headed to see someone by that name. I swear that's all I know."

A sinister smile crossed the human Nekrofiend's pale face. "See, that wasn't so hard, was it? Now it's time I held up my end of the bargain."

His breathing intensified as color began to return to his ghostly thin face. "Oh, praise the Holy Mother. Thank you. Praise be her benevolent word. Wait, why aren't you putting me down? I thought we had a deal?"

"We did. You withheld information from me and that cannot be tolerated."

The color drained from the beggar's face again, and he struggled uselessly to free himself from the tendrils snaked around his wrists. The pale skin around the tendrils grip began to turn red, then bluish-purple from the lack of blood flow.

The man with an endless void for eyes effortlessly ignored his pleas. "Do you know what my enemies call me?" The struggling man was too panicked and continued to babble and mutter curses towards his deity, who likewise ignored his cries. Like the others before him, his shouting at the heavens above was drowned out by the growing shadows around them.

"They call me The Endbringer. Let me show you why."

He closed his eyes, let his head fall back, and raised his arms up, palms facing the skyscrapers above. He focused his mind on his burning hatred of the Aetherial blights that remained. He let it fester—; spreading, consuming, corrupting. He embraced the icy cold Aether as it slithered through his veins down his arms, legs, and chest until it reached the deepest depths of his soul. It gave him strength, control, purpose. He took that purpose, and poured it into the suspended human, willing it to devour the man's essence.

The Endbringer didn't need to see what was in front of him to know exactly what was happening. This wasn't the first time he fed a soul to an Overlord of the Aether, and it wouldn't be his last. The man's veins turned black; his eyes rolled into his head before matching The Endbringer's with their total midnight appearance. The man wretched a handful more times, and a dark crimson dripped out of his tear ducts and from the corner of his mouth. Finally, the Aetherial tendrils released their grip on him, and his body collapsed on the cold steel ground.

The discreet taccom on his wrist vibrated and produced a high-pitch *ding* alerting him to an incoming transmission. It snapped him out of his pleasurable state of mind, and brought back the annoyance from moments ago. "Tobias. Come in Tobias. This is Recruit Second Class Andrew Rodgers"

"Never call me by that name! I demand you address me properly," He hissed at the device.

"Oh, right." The voice cleared his throat then restated his intro-duction. "Are you there, Destroyer of Dreams, Man of Mystery, Dark Wizard of Dark Things, and the ultimate fun-bringer?" Audible cack-ling and roaring laughter cracked through the device from the other end. It raised his anger to a boil, and it took every ounce of restraint he had not to destroy the device and put an end to these fools.

Eventually, the laughing subsided. "Keep making a mockery of me, and I'll show you how I got this name."

"Yeah, okay 'Endbringer'. Anyway, the Emperor wants an audience with you. In person."

"Message received. Inform him I will be on my ship and headed there within the hour."

"Copy that. We'll let him know. Recruit Second Class Rodgers out."

A short *beep* indicated the transmission was over. His Holy Emperor Tenon rarely requested his presence in person, so it must be important. With a few quick presses, he checked to make sure he hadn't missed any other attempts to reach him through calls or messages. Nothing. With a brisk gait, he began walking back to the ship docked a couple of blocks away. Away from this wretched planet filled with debauchery and the deceptive illusion of happiness.

I will find you, Kai Stormbringer. I will find you, and make you wish you never left me to die two decades ago. It's about time we settle the score.

I owe you for that mistake.

| 7 |

Justifying the Means

Approximately one week into Operation: Codename Stormbringer, aboard the Galactic Imperium vessel named Judgement.

"Are you sure this is a good idea? I'm sure we can still pull out of the deal. This doesn't feel right." The fresh recruit protested with wide eyes and an unblemished uniform.

"I'm sure. If you question me one more time, I'm jettisoning you from this damn ship. Is that clear, recruit?" She stared down over her console to her left at the high-back chair the lowly recruit occupied. After silence had passed for a couple of moments, she repeated slower and carefully enunciated every word with vitriol in her voice, eyes still focused on his head, "Is that clear?"

The young man turned around in his chair, big brown eyes wide with fear. His short, matching brown hair gave a stark contrast to the pure white uniform all recruits wore. "Yes, ma'am." He turned around, and pretended to act busy by punching a couple of buttons that amounted to checking the ship's fuel and hull integrity, both insignificant at the time.

Lieutenant Farseer didn't *think* she would actually follow through with the threat, but the temptation was still there. If there was one thing that she learned from watching that brute Captain Demico rise through the ranks, it's that sometimes you have to follow through with a threat or two before people start listening. The trapezoidal viewport in front of them extended the width of the bridge, and nearly the full height of it, too. Among the stars in the distance, they could see a small, crescent-shaped vessel being pummeled with cannon fire as it flew up and over the bow of the assaulting pirate ship. It was fitting, perhaps, that the pirate ship looked like those once described that sailed on watery seas of the ancient Human planet called Earth in the Milky Way galaxy. Though it took their shape, the massive vessel took very little other design choices from it. Likely for the best, considering those primitives barely made it to this galaxy in one piece.

Her mind snapped back to the present, back to the immediate threat at hand. One less Aetherial was one less threat to her Galactic Imperium. Without them, she didn't want to think of where she would be by now. Starving in the "free" streets of Eolian, begging for a piece of bread while everyone blatantly ignores her pleas and casually walks by. The G.I. wasn't perfect, but it was far from the enemy of the people. If anything, the people needed to get out of their way so they could help without constant interference.

A blinding azure flash from the tall bridge of the pirate ship made them all wince, and the recruit frantically pressed button after button on his console. "Their comm system just went offline. I don't know what happened; one minute they were there and now, it's like they vanished." He frantically pushed a bevy of buttons in front of him, trying to re-establish a connection with them. No matter how many he pressed, it would not work.

Farseer knew exactly what happened. The overconfident pirates underestimated the sleek Dominion ship's capabilities. *They must have successfully deployed an E.M.P. blast straight into the bridge. Sneaky bastards, those ones are. Blasted Space Wolves, only good for harassing merchants and causing limited distractions. Definitely not worth the small fortune we had to pay them.*

"Alright, listen up. Change of plans. We are going to do this our-selves. I'm going to take out their engine so they'll be forced to land. That's when the boys and a I will capture the Aetherials so we can transport them back to Aegis Prime. There are plenty of hills on Eolian so unless they crash literally into a city, which I doubt they will, at least not intentionally, we will have the upper hand. Everyone clear?"

A chorus of 'yes ma'am' rang out across the bridge. Every once in a while, it was nice to have the authority and respect of her squad. Any-time that damned Demico monstrosity came around, the mood always changed from sincere respect to pure fear. Though she respected a strong leader, she had seen the aftermath of leading through fear. It wasn't pretty, and never ended well.

She turned to her right and barked orders to the soldier seated in that lower position of the rectangular bridge. "Target their engines with our gatling lasers. No heavy weaponry. We want to damage the ship, not blast it into oblivion. Since we will be catching them off-guard, I doubt they will have rerouted their shields to cover their aft."

A confident male voice replied back from tall soldier with short, blonde hair at whom the new set of orders were directed. "Weapons systems armed and locked on, Lieutenant. T-minus twenty until in range."

Every moment that passed dragged on. Her foot quickly tapped the floor, creating a melodic tin-tin-tin throughout the spacious room. She had no doubt everyone heard the nervous habit, but no one dared to mention it. Not even the new cocky recruit.

A green light illuminated the soldiers face to her right. "We're in range and the target remains in sight. Shall I fire?"

Farseer, without any hesitation that betrayed her nervous foot, said as she nodded her head, "Fire away. Once you disable their engine, fire off a tracking beacon onto their ship. I want to know where it's going if they escape."

To her surprise and annoyance, the recruit turned his head and yelled back over the left of his shoulder. "You sure? If they crash won't that just be a waste of a good tracker-"

"One more word, and I swear by the Holy Mother's blessings I'll toss you out of this ship into the middle of nowhere on Eolian and you'll have to explain to anyone there why they shouldn't shoot you on sight. We all know how much the locals there hate our guts, and would love to make an example of what can happen to a fresh recruit abandoned by his officer."

"Understood. Beginning attack now."

If only Rodriquez were here. She knows I shouldn't need to repeat my order twice before executing it. Damn I miss her.

The man gulped hard, and the lack of color in his face as he turned forward in his seat told her all she needed to know about his continuing lack of obedience. She always prepared for the worst, and even if they failed in capturing them, at least others would know where they were headed next.

As purple flashes of light poured out towards their prey, she admired the beautiful light show. Parts and pieces exploded from the left engine, and it sputtered a few times before its blaze was extinguished. Out of the corner of her eye, she could see her more trusted crew member press a button that launched a tiny claw-like probe towards the ship. It blinked red every so often, something she hoped wouldn't be caught by the enemy before they were apprehended.

Satisfied with her plan, she punched a few buttons on her console. A translucent image of a balding forty-something year old man appeared in front of her. His cheeks were flabby with age, and an unhealthy diet.

"G.I. Intelligence, Officer Anders Fleury here. What can I do for your Lieutenant Farseer?"

"There's a rogue vessel we believe is harboring an Aetherial threat; an old Dominion Crescent class. We are currently following them in a descent to the surface of Eolian. I just hit them with a tracker. I'd like you to keep tabs on it and let us know where they are headed next, should they somehow make an unlikely escape."

It was the slightest of movements, one that most would not have picked up on. Anders Fleury's face lost the blush red on his cheeks and his eyes widened ever so slightly. Farseer prided herself on the ability to pick up on miniscule social ques, and something told her he had prior knowledge of this craft, or those aboard it. She filed that away in her memory as he quickly regained his composure.

"Yes, ma'am. I have it pulled up and will continue tracking it. We will let you know if it leaves Eolian space and where it is headed."

"Thank you, Anders. Mother guide you."

He nodded in return. "And you as well."

The transmission cut off as quickly as it appeared.

As her foot again tapped the metal floor anxiously, she promised herself that after she captured the Aetherial and returned him to Emperor Tenon, she would leave with Rodriguez and get as far away as possible. Whenever doubts about Emperor Tenon's righteous cause crept in as they recently often did, she reminded herself the most important lesson she learned the hard way: *the end always justifies the means.*

I'm coming Rodriguez, just hang on a little bit longer.

| 8 |

Scythe

Two months after the events of Chaos and Consequences

A name is something given at birth, something that uniquely distinguishes one being from any other. They are given out of love, compassion, anger. It's used to call for someone, used when express-ing feelings like passion or disdain, used to refer to a particular being in conversation. As the young Volkoth applied the medipatch to a moderately sized and bloodied gash on his top-left bicep, he enjoyed the echoing shouts after the initial salvo of roaring gunfire while his assailants frantically reloaded their weapons.

He was born an orphan without a home or a name. Though the planet he grew up on was hundreds of lightyears away from this hell-hole, this place still felt all-too familiar. The strangling pressure of the government and their regulations, coupled with the constant threat of "legal" criminal syndicates like the Crimson Skulls, was enough to drive any rational person to the brink of losing their sanity. It's in this type of environment that this particular Volkoth was molded into the being he was today almost twenty-five years later.

The four-armed Volkoth flexed the newly bandaged arm, ensuring the fresh damage would not hinder him from completing this current assignment. A grunt of satisfaction signaled his arm was still working at a satisfactory level. The wall he stood with his back resting against splintered off metal pieces from the gunfire that resumed, inching closer and closer to his two right arms and his midsection.

There had been countless times when he didn't eat for days, when he was barely able to find hydration to keep his body functioning. For years he bounced from street to street in the dingiest parts of Polaria, scrounging for even the tiniest of morsels. It wasn't until he was rescued by a human smuggler that he was given a purpose. That was almost a decade and a half ago, and he still thanked the old gods for him every day he was able to keep breathing.

The two folded scythes on his back were his weapons of choice. He removed them, and as he did so he snapped them forward, sending the blades sliding at a ninety-degree angle before locking into place with a satisfying *click*. He was given this assignment, to send a message to a specific Crimson Skull Underlord, and he wasn't about to let their brawny body guards take him down. He focused his thoughts as time seemed to slow down around him. He felt that familiar pull, that tugging at his instincts that so often throughout recent years guided his scythes and his movements when forced to defend himself.

He opened up his mind and his body to it, and felt the Aether course through him, suspending his light-grey fur in midair as it reached his toes and fingertips. He never thought it was an intelligent being that provided him this power, but he couldn't confirm it wasn't, either. Regardless of where it came from, he was grateful for it. It saved his life dozens of times before, and he didn't doubt it would again today. He understood it was a tool to be used at his discretion, not a weapon to be used carelessly.

His hands taut as they gripped the intricately carved handles of the scythes. He inhaled, and as he exhaled, time nearly froze around him. The plasma bolts and lead bullets continued to relentlessly pummel the wall, though now the debris flying from the assault rocketed by at a snail's pace. He was ready.

The Volkoth emerged from cover, much to the surprise of half a dozen Crimson Skull bodyguards who recovered quickly and resumed their fire, now concentrating on him. Each had the symbolic icon of their crime syndicate, a cracked skull with four crooked teeth and no jawbone tattooed somewhere large and visible on their bodies. One bodyguard had it tattooed on his neck and also painted on his metallic bionic arm. Most wore dark colored pants, and all had tears and stains on their clothing. Compared to the Volkoth approaching them who wore pants that reached to his ankles and a bare, scarred chest, they thought they had the advantage. They were quickly mistaken in that assumption.

He shattered the handles of the scythes together, feeling that familiar locking of mechanisms click into place, with a quarter turn of his wrists, they secured into place. Still walking towards the guards firing wildly at him, he rotated the newly created double-bladed staff counterclockwise, time progressed at a drastically slowed pace for him as he watched bullets and plasma shots float harmlessly past him. Those that were headed for him ricocheted off the whirlwind of scythes; their movement guided and protected by his connection with the Aether. The scythes perfectly deflected the bullets and plasma back at the attackers, striking them with varying degrees of damage. Some writhed in agony from the smoldering holes in their bodies, while others ceased firing for fear of taking more self-inflicted harm.

The raging suppressive fire subsided, until only three Crimson Skull bodyguards were still able to stand; the others twisted in agony from grievous wounds. They charged him with metallic fists and brandished basic, mass-produced swords. The Volkoth was happy to give them a warrior's death, and, with a smile, detached the scythes back into two smaller separate weapons.

He met the first thug head on, ducking to the side to easily avoid the metal fist flying towards him, then countered with a scythe cutting clean through their back. As the two other guards snarled and charged him, the third fell to the floor, limp and lifeless. They stopped short of swinging for him, dropped their weapons, and sprinted past with ghost-while terror painting their faces.

He exhaled, and shook his fur like he was shaking off heavy rainfall as the rush of Aether subsided. The heightened senses, the feeling of control over time, the enjoyable tingling feeling throughout his body, all of it faded away, until it was just him in a metal hallway peppered with bodies and an army of smoking holes from the bullets and plasma.

The warrior stepped over the still bodies and into the office, where a human figure sat in a fancy black chair. The ceiling lights in the room barely lit the desk that sat front and center in the room, with a holovid positioned in the middle of the desk providing better illumination from its blue neon glow. It flickered off as the warrior approached the man, flinging off any remaining blood and gore from his blades before sheathing them on his back in a buttery smooth motion.

"Underlord Redbeard." The Volkoth didn't bother hiding his seething hatred for the man seated in front of him. He was surprisingly tall for a human, and to most he would be extremely intimidating in appearance and stature. Not to this Volkoth, though. The chair he occupied appeared too comfortable for the piece of trash occupying it. He sported a long, orange-red beard with matching long hair flowing past his shoulders, a long gaunt face, and emerald eyes, but any other distinguishing features were difficult to identify in the poor lighting. The only other unique feature were Redbeard's gargantuan arms that reminded him of the specialized biomechanical arms that would allow the wearer to punch holes through Tritanium walls. An empty glass and bottle rested on a nearby circular table.

There was something about Redbeard's eyes. They were augmented with expensive tech, there was no doubt about that. However, it was the way they appeared in the darkness, as if they were the souls of a possessed man. They would have been terrifying to most, but the furry warrior feared nothing in this life, not even death. It came for all, as it had moments ago for this criminal's henchmen.

The crime leader carefully leaned forward, one hand holding a massive flak cannon; the other clenched in a fist. "You took out some of my cheaper bodyguards. I've already requested more and they will be arriving shortly, so you don't have a lot of time. What is it you want?

Clearly, if you were here to kill me, you would have by now." Despite the calm demeanor, the subtle twitches of his left eyelids gave away his frustration at the ease of which his guards were dispatched. It took everything in the Volkoth's body to restrain himself from beheading the arrogant bastard. He reminded himself that he had a mission, and he would complete it. No additional bloodshed was permitted past that which was necessary. That was his code, and he would stick to it.

"The Resistance send their condolences for your guards. We suggest other means besides digging through the scraps of Coropolis, and you may find them more..." he paused for dramatic effect before finishing with "well more alive than these ones." Redbeard squinted, but made no other noticeable movements. "We're tired of playing games. Cease any and all interference with our operations, and we will allow you to continue your reign of gluttonous greed and debauchery."

He considered the peace offering for a moment before agreeing. "I'll see what I can do. You see, I can only speak for myself, and I have no doubt that other Underlords will not find your lackluster offering appetizing. Though, I'll try to keep them away from you, out of good faith, of course."

Stroking his groomed deep-red beard apparently manifested a question from the criminal mastermind. "Before you leave, tell me, mighty Volkoth warrior. What is your name? You look oddly familiar. Have we met before? Surely, we already did our best to recruit someone of your obvious talent."

He turned his head around slightly and grunted in amusement at the audacity of the suggestion. "My name, is Scythe. If we had met before, you have my word that you wouldn't be breathing today. Consider this a first and final warning."

Scythe turn around and left the depressingly dark room without another word, carefully navigating the scattering of bodies he left in his wake. Moments later he was again left to the peace of silence that always came after every battle. It was an odd feeling, surging adrenaline and Aether pumping through his veins, only for it to magically vanish minutes later, as if it had never been there to begin with.

His nostrils flared as he exhaled a relieved breath. It was Underlord Redbeard's lucky day; the Resistance had sent their most obedient warrior to send the message, and he had practiced restraint as part of his craft. The unredeemable villain responsible for his parent's deaths, and that of a myriad of others, should be praying to the old gods and the new for forgiveness and compassion. He wouldn't be shown it again.

His name was Scythe, and though he knew this mission was complete, there was always another waiting for him. He exited the ominous room expecting trouble with his back turned to the ruthless Crimson Skull leader.

It seemed today was also Scythe's lucky day. No flak cannon blast threatened him, only glowing emerald eyes staring creepily as he proceeded out of the building and towards his ship docked in the nearest interstellar hangar.

| 9 |

Just Another Day in Paradise

Seven months after the events of Chaos and Consequences

To most, the arid topography of Vos was pretty much hell. Rainfall was seldom, and when it did come, so did the chance of chemical rain that ate through flesh like a scalding knife through butter. As if that wasn't welcoming enough, there were the occasional ravenous beasts that ventured too close to settled territory. So, yeah, hell wasn't too far off base as an accurate description for most.

Greymore Sky wasn't most people though.

A self-anointed Protector, he tasked himself with guarding those in their small town. He was just one person, but someone had to look out for the elderly, young, and feeble. No one else volunteered for the job, so he volunteered himself; he would be the one to take up that position. An unlimited cache of booze made the long days and short nights more bearable.

Just another day, Greymore thought as he checked the extended clip on his Mk. II Asaki Plasma Rifle and flipped off the safety. The weapon belched to life, atoms smashed together and produced a stunning orange glow from the chamber roughly halfway down the gun, perfectly centered between the barrel and the handcrafted metal stock. It gave off an eerie luminosity that he would have admired, if not for the reason he was out this late at night, or early in the morning, however you looked at it. The early Asaki line of rifles weren't pretty to look at, but they were damned reliable, and that's what he needed. Something to rely on. With an Aether Core melded into it, he knew he could trust the firearm to get the job done, whatever and whenever it was.

He aimed down the sight, waiting for the perfect moment to let loose a volley of deadly molten liquid into the intruder. A puff of breath out the side of his mouth blew aside stray white hairs that threatened to obstruct his view, and that would only lead to a quick, untimely end for the Protector. The only one Death was coming for tonight was the unknown interloper.

Greymore removed his eye from the sight. Scanning the horizon with it for the last couple of minutes hadn't revealed the threat. It had to be somewhere. He *knew* it was somewhere. His heavy sleep was never disturbed unless something threatened the village—Or him.

He closed his eyes and cleared his mind, forcing all thoughts down into the depths of his consciousness. One deep breath in. Exhale. A second deep breath in. Exhale. A third deep breath in. Pause. Long exhale. One second passed, one second and ten milliseconds, one second and twenty milliseconds.

There! He didn't see it yet, but since his eyes weren't getting better with age, he learned to rely on other means to do his duty as Protector. Thankfully, his other senses remained sharp, and they kept him alive. For now, at least. He pivoted thirty degrees to his left and raised the rifle again. His mind still clear, he extended his senses out, his bare feet shifted slightly for a sturdier stance. The calloused soles wore years of wear and tear, yet still remained sensitive to any vibrations in the cracked dirt underneath.

Miles off, he felt multiple vibrations. Pounding hooves kicked up a massive cloud of dust behind them. A family of brown-bellied bull-lions charged for the town. Their black coats of fur covered their six legs and massive feline bodies, with their bellies featuring a leathery brown skin. Short curved horns protruded on the top of their lion-like heads that had puffy manes, while the females shared the same characteristics minus the horns and manes. They were predators to a lot of the sparse wildlife and settlers on Vos, but tonight they were prey. That could only mean one thing: something much bigger and meaner was on their tails, and it was headed straight for the town.

He knew he had to act quick before they got too close. He reached for a small metal device in a pocket on his belt, and retrieved it. Holding the triangular thing to his mouth, he blew into a perfectly shaped hole on one side. To any normal human ear, the pitch was inaudible. To bull-lions though, it sounded like the wicked screams of a wounded member of their herd. Greymore hoped it would be enough to drive them in any other direction except the one they were headed.

Distant roars rumbled across the gap between them, and through the magnified scope he could see the cloud turn ninety degrees to its right and continue away from the small village. As the cloud shrunk, he still felt something wasn't right. They weren't running towards something; they had been running away from something. His senses warned him that something big and nasty, and racing towards him.

Again, he extended his senses. His calloused feet searching for the source of the disturbance and a possible path it might be taking. Deep underground, something stirred the earth. It undulated as it moved soil and rock, sending shockwaves of vibration that he could feel throughout his entire body now. It drew close, and it was massive.

This must have been what spooked those bull-lions. Come on, you big gnarly bastard. I've got a surprise for you right here. I've handled my fair share of your kind, and all but one has been nothing more than a minor nuisance.

The ground trembled under him, the intensity of it nearly knocking him off his feet. A few hundred feet away the dirt burst into the air, and in the plume of dust and debris towered a beast he hoped he would never see in person again. They were a rare breed of wurm, one that can devour small one-pilot space ships in a single lunge. Their bold navy scales also protected it against a variety of projectiles. It's only known weakness: the eight blinking eyes on the front of its long, cylindrical form. Half a dozen rows of dagger-like teeth gnashed together in a deadly maw waiting to devour flesh.

Inhale. Exhale. He took another deep breath, then exhaled slowly as the creature bellowed a nightmarish roar that shook the earth as much as its movement. Greymore closed his eyes, searching for that center of focus he knew was there. He had suppressed it for a long time, but that fiery focus still burned, even as dim as he kept the candle lit. It was there. It was *always* there.

Hello, old friend. Oh, how I've missed you. I know we didn't always agree, but I hope you won't mind one more dance with the devil.

As he opened his eyes from his trance, he saw the creature hit the ground with incredible force and begin slithering towards him. Its gaping mouth gnashed hungrily the whole time it approached. His eyes flickered and began emitting an eerily similar glow to the one still coming from within the center of the rifle he held. He poured more focus into the central chamber of it, and its glow became a beacon of orange brilliance.

A twisted smile crept up the corner of his mouth as he whispered, "not on my watch, pal." He relished the exhilaration of the fight. Man versus monster. It was a classic story, and one to which he always enjoyed writing the ending. So far, he had been able to walk away and tell the tale of his victorious conclusions.

To most, Vos was a desolate wasteland, but to Greymore, it was far more.

Today is just another day in paradise. And he wouldn't have it any other way.

By day, he's a cybersecurity professional. By night, he's the author of the Aetherial War series. As an avid lover of science fiction and fantasy stories, Nathan grew up mesmerized by Star Wars, and hoped that one day he could create a universe as entertaining and fascinating as Mr. George Lucas. Now, he's proud to say he has been able to live his dreams among the stars, and hopes others will share his passion and excitement for all the stories to come in the Aetherial War universe. Nathan is also the proud founder and owner of the card and board game publisher Creative Mind Games LLC, where he is actively creating the official Aetherial War Card Game based on characters and events from the series.

For more information, you can visit www.aetherialwar.com to read exciting lore from the Aetherial War universe, or even check out the official card game.